OUR SHED

A Father-Daughter Building Story

ROBERT BRODER

Illustrated by
CARRIE O'NEILL

little bigfoot
an imprint of sasquatch books
seattle, wa

Manufactured in China by C&C Offset Printing Co. Ltd.
Shenzhen, Guangdong Province, in December 2020

LITTLE BIGFOOT with colophon is a registered trademark
of Penguin Random House LLC

25 24 23 22 21   9 8 7 6 5 4 3 2 1

Editors: Christy Cox, Michelle McCann
Production editor: Bridget Sweet
Designer: Anna Goldstein

Library of Congress Cataloging-in-Publication Data
Names: Broder, Robert, author. | O'Neill, Carrie, illustrator.
Title: Our shed : a father-daughter building story / Robert Broder ;
   illustrations by Carrie O'Neill.
Description: Seattle, WA : Little Bigfoot, [2020] | Audience: Ages 5-7. |
   Audience: Grades K-1. | Summary: A father teaches his daughter
   about woodworking and she contributes imagination and fun as
   they build a shed together.
Identifiers: LCCN 2019052877 | ISBN 9781632172648 (hardcover)
Subjects: CYAC: Sheds--Fiction. | Carpentry--Fiction. |
   Imagination--Fiction.
Classification: LCC PZ7.1.B75756 Our 2020 | DDC [E]--dc23
LC record available at https://lccn.loc.gov/2019052877

ISBN: 978-1-63217-264-8

Sasquatch Books
1904 Third Avenue, Suite 710
Seattle, WA 98101
SasquatchBooks.com

For my dad. —RB

To Agnes and Imogen. And in loving
memory of my dad. —CO

Dad and I are planning to build a shed in our backyard.

"Why do we need a shed?" I ask.

"To put things in," he answers.

"What kind of things?" I ask.

"Sleds, bikes, garden tools, lawn mower . . . or should we bring the lawn mower into the living room?"

"No," I say.

"That's why we need a shed," he replies.

First we go to the hardware store.
We buy nails, screws, hinges, and a latch.
Dad lets me pick out the latch.

Next we go to the lumberyard
to choose the wood.

He shows me how to check each board to make sure it's not warped.

Before heading home, we stop for lunch at our favorite diner.

Finally, we unload the wood and supplies
and carry them into the backyard.

I tap dance on the wood like it's my own private dance floor.

Dad grins and joins
me for some twirls.

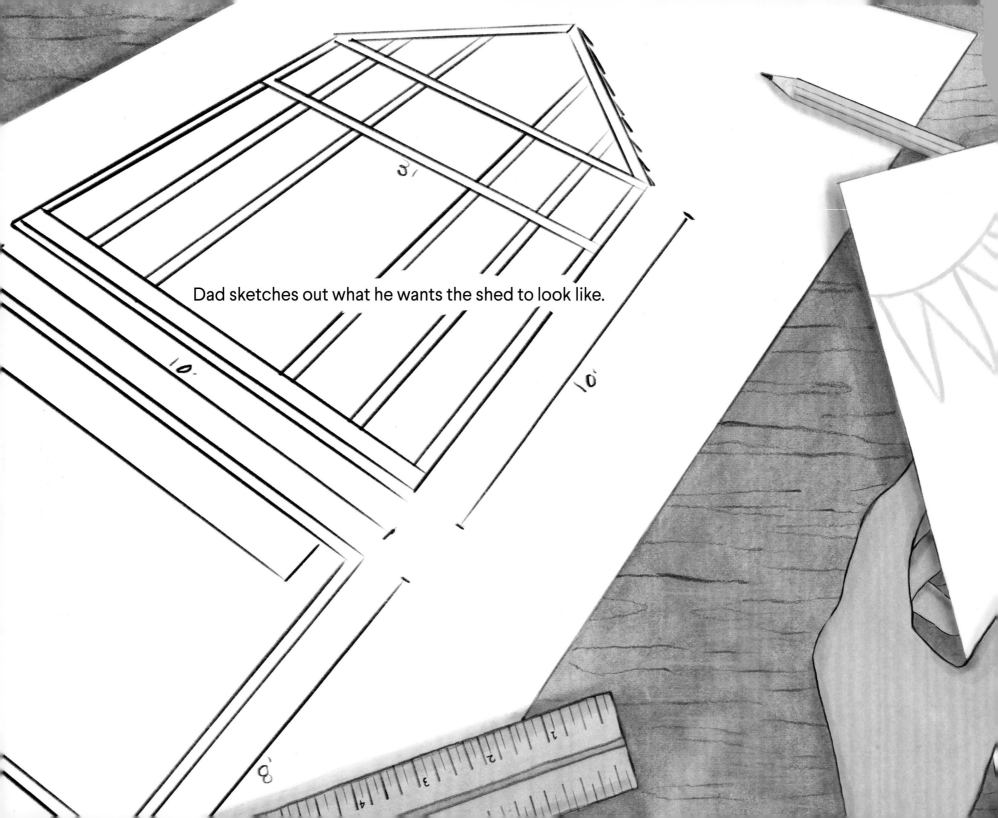

Dad sketches out what he wants the shed to look like.

I sketch out my own plan.

He lays the boards across the sawhorses and starts measuring.

"Measure twice, cut once," Dad tells me. "That way you know your board is the right size."

I use the level to make sure the wood is straight as he cuts it.

I also use the saw. Dad shows me how to safely use the knuckle of my thumb as a guide, to help the cut stay straight.

We frame the shed and put up the walls.

We take a break and I battle the nastiest dragon in the land.

"En garde!" I shout.

The daddy-dragon roars as if he's breathing fire.

I block the fire with all my might.

After defeating the beast, I hand Dad the nails when he asks for them. I check the boards with the level to make sure everything is straight.

Building our shed takes us three days. When it's done—and the hinges are on and the latch is attached—it is time to paint.

Dad lets me pick the color.

"I can't decide!" I say.

"Let's get both!" Dad declares.

We stop at our favorite deli and
order sandwiches to go.

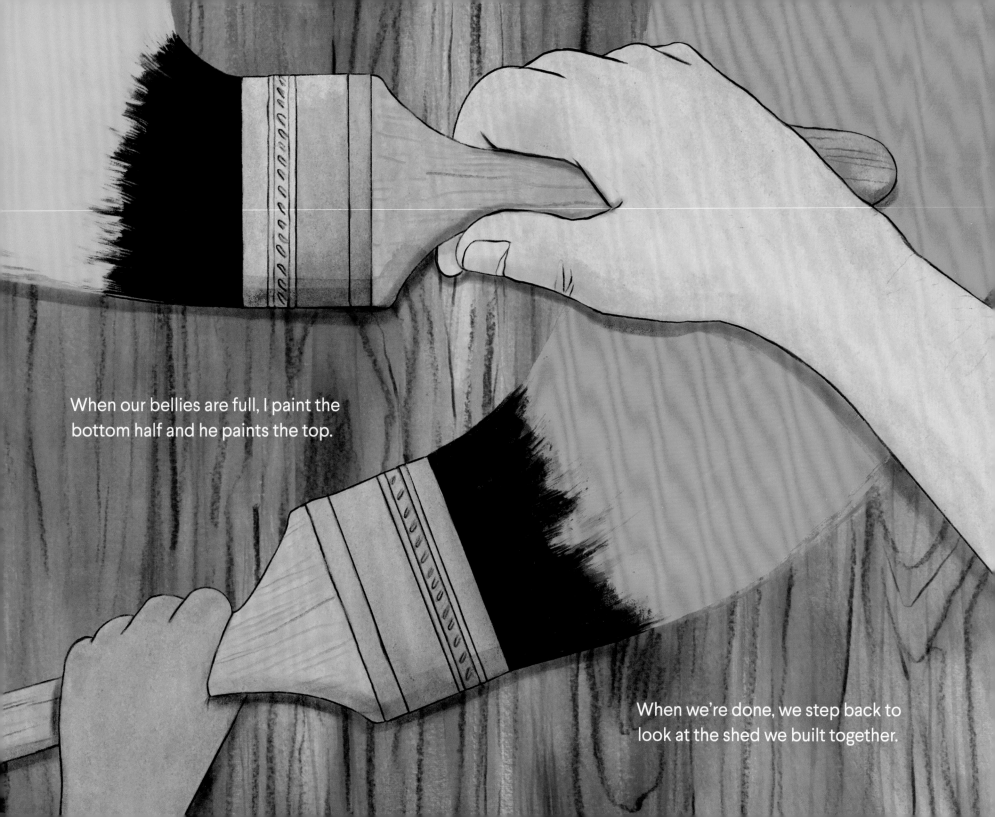

When our bellies are full, I paint the bottom half and he paints the top.

When we're done, we step back to look at the shed we built together.

I squint. "It looks a little crooked."

Dad squints too. "Hmph! It does look crooked."

"But it feels sturdy," Dad says. "I don't expect this shed to fall down anytime soon. Besides, crooked is good. It helps keep the dragons away."

Dad was right.

Through the years, the shed sat in our backyard—along with a family of mice who lived in the top corner of the shed and kept to themselves.

In the spring, we brought out our bird feeder and bikes.

In the summer, we grabbed our sidewalk chalk and sprinkler.

In the fall, we pulled out the wheelbarrow and rakes.

And in the winter, we hauled out
our snow shovels and sleds.

Through all the seasons of wind and rain and
sun and snow, our shed's paint started to fade.

"Why are we painting the shed?" my son asks.

"Because it's time," I answer.

When we are done, we stand back to look at the shed.

My son squints. "It looks a little crooked," he says.

I squint too. "Yes, but it feels sturdy," I say. "I don't expect our shed to fall down anytime soon. Besides, crooked is good. It will help keep the dragons out."

"En garde!"